THIS WALKER BOOK BELONGS TO:

_____

_____

_____

For James

and Rebecca

With thanks to the Manhattan Toy Company who allowed
their Floppy Bunny © to appear in this book.

First published 1997 by
Walker Books Ltd, 87 Vauxhall Walk
London SE11 5HJ

This edition published 2004 for Index Books Ltd

6 8 10 9 7

This book has been typeset in Berkeley Old Style

Printed in China

British Library Cataloguing in Publication Data:
a catalogue record for this book
is available from the British Library

ISBN 0-7445-6338-0

www.walkerbooks.co.uk

Friends

Kim Lewis

WALKER BOOKS
AND SUBSIDIARIES
LONDON • BOSTON • SYDNEY

Sam's friend Alice came to play on the farm. They were in the garden when they heard loud clucking coming from the hen house.

"Listen!" said Sam. "That means a hen has laid an egg."

"An egg!" said Alice. "Let's go and find it."

Sam and Alice
ran to the
hen house.

"Look," said Alice. "There's the egg!"

"I can put it in my hat," said Sam.

"I can put your hat in my bucket,"
said Alice, "and put the bucket
in the wheelbarrow."

"Then we can take it home,"
said Sam.

The geese stood across the path.

"I'm afraid of geese," said Alice.

"Come on," said Sam. "We can go the long way round."

Alice pushed the wheel-
barrow through the trees.
"It's my turn now," said
Sam, and he pulled it
through the long grass
and thistles.

Together, they lifted it
over a ditch.

Sam and Alice went into the barn.

They were followed by Glen, the old farm dog.

"Is the egg all right?" asked Alice.

Sam and Alice
looked in the hat.
The egg was safe
and smooth,
without a crack.
"Look what we've found!"
said Alice, holding out
the egg to Glen.
"No!" cried Sam.
"He'll eat it!"

Sam reached out to take the egg.
Alice held it tight.
"It's mine!" said Sam.
"It's not!" said Alice. "I found it!"
"They're my hens!" said Sam,
pushing Alice.

SMASH went the egg as it fell on the ground. Glen started to eat it.

"I don't like you any more," said Alice. She picked up her bucket and went out of the barn.

Sam put on his empty hat. He did like Alice and he didn't like Alice and he felt he was going to cry.

Just then loud clucking
came from the hen house.
Sam ran out of the barn.
"Another egg!" he cried.
Sam and Alice looked at
each other.
"We can go and find it,"
said Sam.
"Yes, let's!" said Alice,
and smiled.

Sam put the egg
in his hat. He gave
the hat to Alice who
put it in her bucket.
They tiptoed past the geese and
Glen and walked back
to the house.

"What have you two been doing?" asked Mum.

"Finding eggs," said Sam.

"Together!" said Alice.

WALKER BOOKS is the world's leading independent publisher of children's books. Working with the best authors and illustrators we create books for all ages, from babies to teenagers – books your child will grow up with and always remember. So…

FOR THE BEST CHILDREN'S BOOKS, LOOK FOR THE BEAR